THE TALKING MICKEY MOUSE SHOW™

A Moose
on the
Loose

WORLDS OF WONDER™

Printed in U.S.A.   ISBN: 1-55578-306-6

Mickey   I'll never forget the ski trip Goofy and I took to Canada. I couldn't wait to hit the slopes! But on the drive up there, Goofy was a little worried…

Goofy   Gawrsh, Mick, I've never tried this before. When I'm up on the mountain, what if I slip?

Mickey   You're supposed to slip. That's the whole idea.

Goofy   You are?

Mickey Sure. You go to the top of the mountain, then you slip and slide all the way down. It's called skiing.

Goofy Skiing, huh? You know, I think I *have* done it before.

Mickey That's great, Goofy. Where?

Goofy In my bathtub!

Mickey Look, Goofy, there's the ski lodge up ahead. We're almost there!

Mickey When we got to the lodge, Goofy noticed something strange.

Goofy That's funny. Hardly anyone's on the slopes. They're all at the lodge.

Mickey Gee, they seem kind of mad. Just listen to them.

Man That animal scared us to death! You're the manager, Mrs. North. Can't you do something?

North Please, please! I've done everything I can!

Mickey	Excuse me, Mrs. North. I'm Mickey Mouse, and this is my friend Goofy. What's wrong?
North	Oh, it's just terrible. A giant moose has been chasing skiers all over the mountain.
Goofy	You mean there's a moose on the loose?
North	Yes, I'm afraid he's going to hurt someone. And now everyone's so worried, they won't go skiing!
Man	You'd better believe we won't! We're not going to stand for this any more!

Mickey The man stomped off and the other skiers followed. Mrs. North looked pretty discouraged.

North It's been like this all week. Wouldn't you know it would happen just when my husband was out of town.

Goofy How long has the moose been here?

North Long enough to chase away a lot of guests. If he keeps scaring away business, we could lose our jobs here. We can't let that happen—not with Alice.

Mickey Who's Alice?

North Come into my office and I'll show you.

North	See? Here she is.
Goofy	Mick, it's a pretty little baby. Goofy-Goofy-Goo.
Mickey	Isn't that goochy-goochy-goo?
Goofy	That's not what my momma said to me!
Mickey	Mrs. North, I didn't know there were moose in this part of Canada.
North	There usually aren't. This one must have got lost and wandered onto our mountain.
Mickey	Well, don't worry. One way or another, Goofy and I will take care of that moose. We're not going to let Alice's parents lose their job.

Mickey Goofy and I decided that the first thing to do was go see the moose for ourselves. We found him the same way everybody else did—by going skiing.

Goofy Whoa! I take it all back, Mick. This is nothing like my bathtub.

Mickey Hang in there, Goofy.

Goofy You know, maybe I should try skiing on my knees.

Mickey On your knees? Why's that?

Goofy 'Cause then I wouldn't have so far to fall!

Mickey	Goofy, look, there's the moose. And he doesn't seem too happy!
Goofy	He's coming this way! Now what'll we do?
Mickey	We get out of his way! And fast!
Goofy	I—I can't move! Oh, doggone these skis. I'm just going to take them off and run!
Mickey	And that's just what Goofy did. He must have been pretty scared, because he passed me in just a few seconds!

Mickey   Goofy scrambled up a tree, and I was right behind him. The moose stood below, making an awful racket.

Goofy   That moose is crazy!

Mickey   We're the crazy ones—for trying to find him in the first place.

Goofy   Say, Mick, I've got a question for you. If two gooses are called geese, are two mooses called meese?

Mickey	No, two mooses are called moose. Goofy, do you really think that's important at a time like this?
Goofy	Hm, I guess not. Okay, I've got a question that really is important.
Mickey	What's that, Goof?
Goofy	Can moose climb trees?
Mickey	I hope not, Goofy. I sure hope not.

Mickey   We found out that they can't climb trees, because after a while our moose gave up and wandered off.

Goofy   When the coast was clear, Mickey and I climbed down and headed back to the lodge.

Mickey   Well, Goofy, we still haven't done anything to help Mrs. North. I just wish we could figure out why that moose is so grumpy.

Goofy   I guess I'd be grumpy too if I was stuck on a mountain all by myself.

Mickey   Goofy, what did you just say?

Goofy   Gee, Mick…I can't remember.

Mickey   You said the moose was all by himself. That's the answer! I'll bet he's lonely.

Goofy   I'm sorry, but I'm not going back up there to visit.

Mickey   Not lonely for people—lonely for meese! I mean, moose!

Goofy   But Mick, you heard what the lady said—there aren't any others around here.

Mickey   We'll see what we can do about that. Come on, Goofy!

Goofy	As soon as we got back to the lodge we started on Mickey's plan.
Mickey	We needed some room to spread out, so Mrs. North let us use the floor of her office.
Goofy	Look, Mick. Little Alice is crawling around trying to help. Goofy-Goofy-Goo!
Mickey	I sure hope my plan works, Goofy.
Goofy	Me, too. Those skiers are getting more upset by the minute!

Man   Did you get rid of that moose yet, Mrs. North? My wife and I are sure tired of watching TV!

North   It's being taken care of right now, sir. A special team of moose-busters is working on it at this very moment!

Goofy   Moose-busters! Hey, Mick, we can stop. She hired some experts!

Mickey   Sorry to break it to you, Goofy...but I'm afraid *we're* the experts.

Mickey	By the time we finished, the guests at the lodge were parading around with signs, demanding their money back. Before we left, we said goodbye to Mrs. North.
North	What's in the boxes, Goofy?
Goofy	You'll see—and so will the moose!
North	Well, good luck. And be careful!
Mickey	Come on, Goofy, up the slopes!
Goofy	On skis again? I don't know if I can make it.
Mickey	Just this one last time, Goof. Then you can do all your skiing in the bathtub.

Mickey Well, Goofy, here's the top of the mountain…and you're still on your feet.

Goofy The top of the mountain? Shucks, I hardly recognized it standing rightside up.

Mickey Wait, I see something coming over the rise…antlers!

Goofy Whew! I thought for a minute there it might be the moose.

Mickey It is the moose! Quick, let's open these boxes!

Goofy My fingers are shakin' so bad I can hardly get the top off.

Mickey Just remember, Goofy, that moose is lonely. He's looking for a friend.

Goofy I wish he'd look somewhere else!

Mickey We opened the boxes and pulled out what we'd been working on—a moose costume! It was hard to put it on while we were still wearing skis.

Goofy Hey Mick, can I be the front instead of the back?

Mickey Why, Goofy?

Goofy 'Cause I can't see a thing in here!

Mickey It's too late now. Here he comes! Okay, Goofy, act friendly!

Goofy Tell *him* that!

Mickey Wait a minute, the moose is stopping! He's not angry. He's—he's glad to see us!

Goofy   How can you tell? Is he waggin' his tail?

Mickey   He's smiling! I never thought I'd see a moose smile.

Goofy   I still haven't. It's dark in here!

Mickey   Our plan worked, Goofy! Now he's running this way!

Goofy   But he's happy, right?

Mickey   Yeah, but he's going to smash right into us! Brace yourself!

Goofy   Whoaa!

Goofy   What's happenin', Mick? How come we're movin'?

Mickey   We're sliding down the hill. Hold on tight!

Goofy   Yeow! W-well, at least we're gettin' away from that moose.

Mickey   Guess again, Goofy. He's right behind us.

Goofy   What's in front of us?

Mickey   Nothing much, just a tree. A tree! Lean to the left, Goofy!

Goofy   Whoaa!

Mickey   Oh, no, a big rock. Lean to the right! Just missed!

Goofy   Mick, I'm tired of bein' a moose. Can we go back to the lodge now?

Mickey   That's exactly where we're going. It's straight ahead!

Mickey   Down below, Mrs. North saw us coming.

North   Look, Alice, someone's skiing. This is crazy—it's a moose. And there's another moose right behind it! Oh, no, I wish Mickey and Goofy were here!

Mickey   Meanwhile, Goofy and I wished we *weren't* there.

Goofy   Mick, you don't mean the lodge is *straight* ahead, do you?

Mickey   I'm afraid so, Goofy! Come on, let's steer to the right. Lean like you've never leaned before!

Mickey   We leaned so far that we started tumbling. The costume came apart and my moose head flew off. The next thing we knew, we were sitting in a snowbank.

Goofy   Mick, we made it. And I can see!

Mickey   Unfortunately, so can that moose…and he sees that we tricked him.

Goofy   Nice moose. Nice Mr. Moose. Mick, he's not smilin' anymore.

Goofy	Hey, Mick, what's that next to the moose?
Mickey	Oh, no, it's Alice! She crawled right up to him!
North	Mickey, Goofy! Please, help my baby!
Goofy	Uh-oh, the moose just saw Alice.
Mickey	Quick, Goofy, we've got to save her!
Goofy	I can't, Mick. I'm stuck in this costume.
Mickey	Me, too. Oh, no, this is terrible!

Goofy   I can't look. What happened?

Mickey   I don't believe it. Alice is petting the moose...and he's nuzzling her right back! Why, he's even smiling.

North   Come on, Alice. Come back to Mommy. Isn't that a nice moose?

Mickey   We thought the moose just needed a friend. But the friend he needed wasn't us—it was Alice. I think maybe Mrs. North's problems are over.

Mickey   The next day, the skiers were back on the slopes, and Goofy and I were ready to go home.

Goofy   Mrs. North, it's been a pleasure stayin' at your lodge—except for being chased by that moose.

North   Well, Goofy, the moose won't be chasing people anymore...now that he's got a friend. He seems happy to live in the woods down here by the lodge.

Goofy   Yup, he's gentle as a...as a...

Mickey   As a baby. Right, Alice?

North   Mickey, I just want to thank you and Goofy for all your help. You're welcome back anytime.

Goofy   No offense, ma'am, but we may not be back for a while. I think we'll go water skiing next time.

Mickey   Water skiing?

Goofy   That's right, Mick. After all, moose can't swim...can they?

PINEY PEAK
SKI LODGE